Five Little Mermaids

written by Sunny Scribens

illustrated by Barbara Vagnozzi

sung by Audra Mariel

Five little mermaids
Went swimming in the sea
To the **Atlantic Ocean**
To see what they could see.

Maria joined a **school** of fish
And swam away carefree.
Whoosh!
Now there were . . .

Makaiya met a **turtle**
And forgot the other three.
Bye!
Now there were . . .

Three little mermaids
Swimming in the sea
To the **Southern Ocean**
To see what they could see.

Ming high-fived a **penguin**
And swam away with glee.
Splash!
Now there were . . .

TWO little mermaids
Swimming in the sea
To the Pacific Ocean
To see what they could see.

Marley saw a **giant squid**
And turned around to flee.
Aaaaah!
Now there was . . .

One little mermaid
swimming in the sea
To the **Arctic Ocean**
To see what she could see.

Maya saw a **jellyfish**
And went off to sightsee.
Wow!
Now there were *no* little mermaids
Swimming in the sea.

So many mermaids
Swimming in the seas
Sharing their stories
With their mermaid families!

When they get together
It's as fun as can be.
Yeah!
It's time for a party in the sea!

More About Mermaids!

What Is a Mermaid?

Mermaids are imaginary creatures who are part-human and part-fish. There are stories about mermaids who live in all kinds of water: oceans, rivers, lakes, ponds and even oases in the desert. Mermaids are often female, but tales also describe mermen. Merpeople or merfolk can be any gender.

Mermaids Around the World

The word mermaid comes from Middle English, the language that people living in England spoke many hundreds of years ago. They combined the words **mere** ("sea") and **mayde** ("girl"). There are different words for mermaid in every language, because cultures all over the world have their own stories about fish-people. Here are just a few!

Greece:
In Greek stories from thousands of years ago, mermaids called **nereids** live in an underwater palace and sometimes offer help to sailors. In Greek art, mermaids appear as humans covered in fish scales.

Japan:
Ningyo are part-fish part-human creatures from Japanese legends (very old and important stories). In these stories, eating ningyo can bring health and long life, but can also cause terrible storms and bad luck.

Are Mermaids Real?

dugong →

Throughout history, various people including sailors and pirates have claimed to see mermaids. Most scientists think that these people actually saw sea cows, which are real ocean creatures. There are two types of sea cow: manatees and dugongs. Sea cows look a little like humans because they swim using two flippers like arms to paddle.

Central America:

The tales of Tupi and Guaraní people describe a water queen named **Iara** with dark skin and green algae-covered hair. Stories say that people can follow her strong singing voice to her underwater home.

New Zealand:

In the legends of the Māori people, creatures who live in lakes or rivers are called **taniwha**. Taniwha can help keep people safe, or they can trick and hurt humans. Taniwha who live in the sea are called **marakihau**.

West, Central and Southern Africa:

Many different African cultures have stories about a goddess who can control water. **Mami Wata** is a name people use for any goddess like this. When Mami Wata appears in art, she often has snakes wound around her body. Like in other mermaid tales, she can bring great luck or terrible danger.

Five Oceans

The oceans in this book are actually five connected parts of one huge global ocean. Scientists have found and named about 250,000 species of life in these salty waters, and they think that there might be up to 750,000 more.

The Largest Ocean

The **Pacific Ocean** is larger than all of the land on Earth combined! It holds about half of the Earth's water. Around the Pacific Ocean is the Ring of Fire, an area where most of the planet's biggest earthquakes and volcanic eruptions happen. The deepest point of the Pacific Ocean is called the Mariana Trench. All of Mount Everest could fit under water there — and the top of the mountain would still be 2 miles (3.2km) below the water's surface.

The Warmest Ocean

For the past hundred years, the **Indian Ocean** has been warming up faster than any other ocean. Scientists believe that this warming is part of climate change caused by humans. Warmer water makes it hard for tiny animals called plankton to survive, which means it is also harder for fish that eat plankton to find enough food. Ocean warming might also cause changes in the strong winds, called monsoons, that bring storms to Asia.

The Coldest Ocean

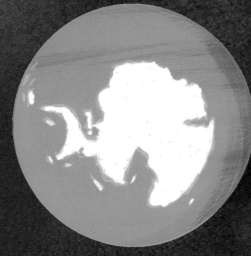

It is hard for people to sail ships in the **Southern Ocean** because it has very strong winds and cold temperatures. The winds blow hard enough to move water all the way around Antarctica. This moving water is called the Antarctic Circumpolar Current. Water from the Pacific, Atlantic and Indian Oceans combines in this current and flows into the Southern Ocean.

The Saltiest Ocean

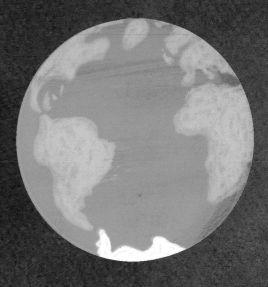

The Mid-Atlantic Ridge is an underwater mountain range that divides the **Atlantic Ocean** into two pieces. The highest points of the Mid-Atlantic Ridge reach out of the water to form volcanic islands, like Þingvellir in Iceland. Many ships travel across the Atlantic between the Americas, Europe and Africa, but icebergs and hurricanes can make those journeys dangerous.

The Smallest Ocean

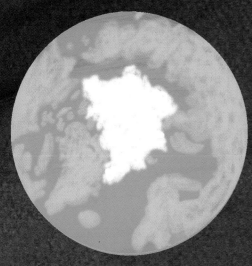

Sea ice covers much of the **Arctic Ocean**, providing a home for arctic animals like polar bears. In the winter, there can be twice as much sea ice over the Arctic Ocean as there is in the summer. Climate change has caused a lot more sea ice than usual to melt, which makes it harder for arctic animals to find food and homes.

Creatures in This Book...

Lion's Mane Jellyfish

Some people think that the thin, hair-like tentacles of this jellyfish look like a lion's mane. The longest one anyone has ever seen washed up on the shore of the Massachusetts Bay in 1870. Its tentacles were 120ft (37m) long — which makes it longer than a blue whale!

66 feet (20 m)

Emperor Penguin

Penguins are birds with flippers instead of wings, and they swim rather than fly. Emperor penguins can dive deeper than any other bird and stay underwater to feed for more than 20 minutes. To warm up outside the water, they huddle together in groups. Each penguin takes a turn in the middle, then moves to the outside to give the next penguin their chance to get warm.

1,850 feet (564 m)

Giant Squid

Scientists don't know a lot about giant squids because they live so deep in the ocean. It is very hard for people to go that far down below the surface of the water. In 2012, using a special underwater vehicle with a super-sensitive camera, scientists in Japan took the first video of a giant squid in its natural habitat.

3,300 feet (1,006 m)

and How Deep They Can Swim!

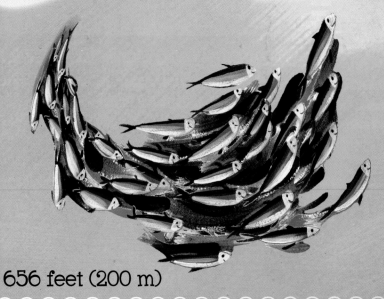

School of Herring

There are more herring in the world than almost any other type of fish. There are over 200 kinds of herring, and female herring can lay up to 40,000 eggs at a time. Their silver scales help them stay hidden from predators, because when their scales shine they look like light shining in the water.

656 feet (200 m)

Sea Turtle

Sea turtles have existed on Earth for more than 110 million years, since the time of the dinosaurs. Unlike other turtles, they cannot pull their legs and heads back into their shells. The leatherback, the only kind of sea turtle that does not have a hard shell, can dive the deepest.

3,000 feet (914 m)

Five Little Mermaids

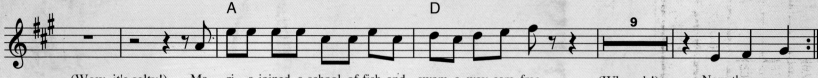

Five lit-tle mer-maids went swim-ming in the sea To the At-lan-tic O-cean to see what they could see.

(Wow, it's salty!) Ma-ri-a joined a school of fish and swam a-way care-free. (Whoosh!) Now there were...

For Sasha — S. S.

To Daniel and Alexander, to whom I read so many
stories from Barefoot Books when they were little — B. V.

Barefoot Books
2067 Massachusetts Ave
Cambridge, MA 02140

Barefoot Books
29/30 Fitzroy Square
London, W1T 6LQ

Graphic design by Sarah Soldano, Barefoot Books
Edited and art directed by Lisa Rosinsky, Barefoot Books
Reproduction by Bright Arts, Hong Kong
Printed in China on 100% acid-free paper
This book was typeset in Carrotcake,
Chalkboard, Kidprint and Yourz Truly Regular
The illustrations were prepared in
acrylics and colored pencils

Text copyright © 2019 by Sunny Scribens
Illustrations copyright © 2019 by Barbara Vagnozzi
The moral rights of Sunny Scribens and
Barbara Vagnozzi have been asserted

Lead vocals by Audra Mariel
Musical arrangement © 2019 by Mike Flannery
Produced, mixed and mastered at
Jumping Giant, New York City, USA
Animation by Sophie Marsh, Bristol, UK

Hardback with enhanced CD ISBN 978-1-78285-831-7
Paperback with enhanced CD ISBN 978-1-78285-832-4
E-book ISBN 978-1-78285-864-5

British Cataloguing-in-Publication Data: a catalogue record
for this book is available from the British Library

Library of Congress Cataloging-in-Publication Data
is available upon request

First published in United States of America
by Barefoot Books, Inc and in Great Britain
by Barefoot Books, Ltd in 2019

135798642